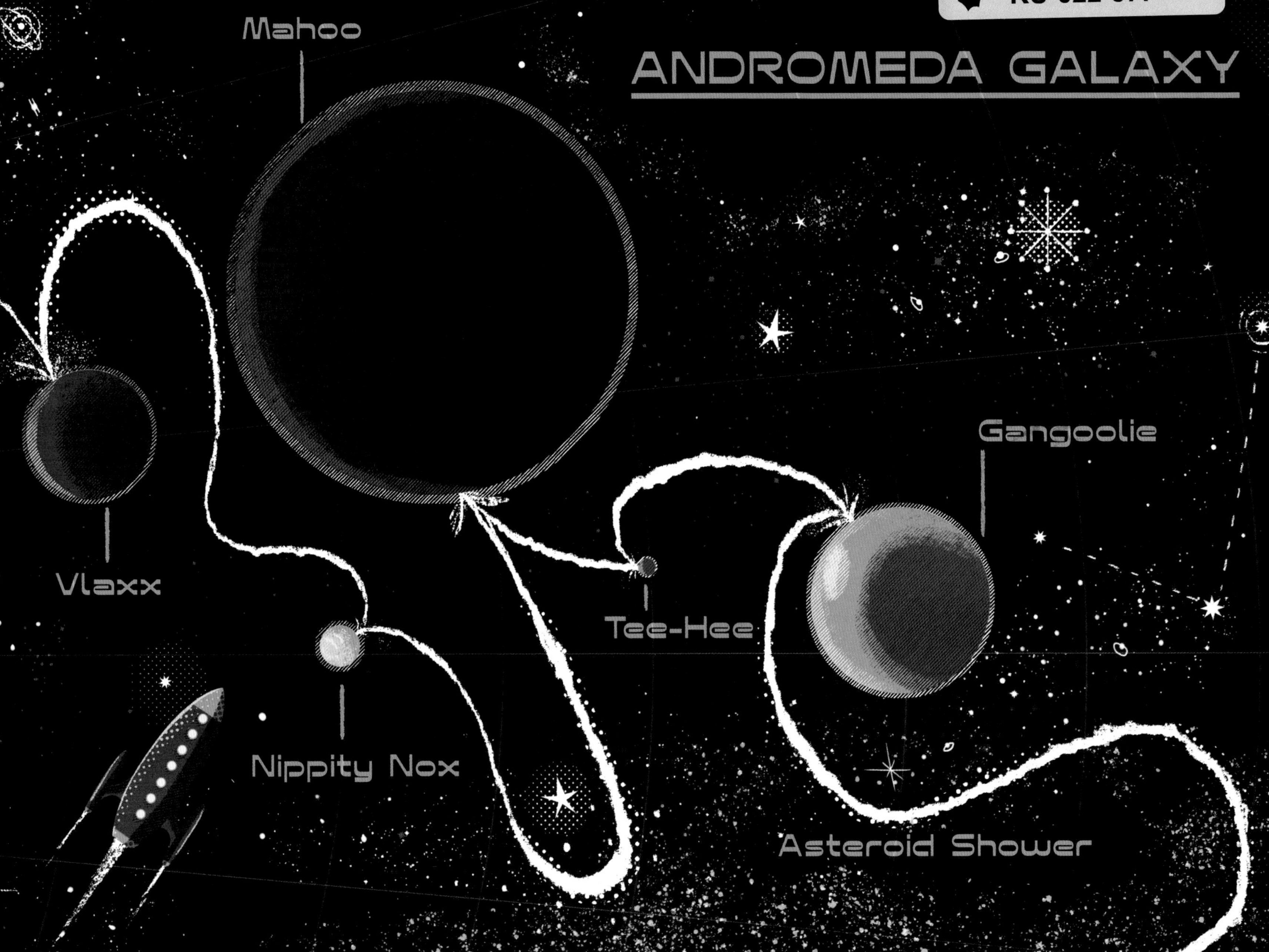


CANIS MAJOR DWARF GALAXY

Hey-Diddle-Diddle

For Lucy – P B

For Josie – C J

HODDER CHILDREN'S BOOKS
First published in Great Britain in 2020 by Hodder and Stoughton

1 3 5 7 9 10 8 6 4 2

 A CIP catalogue record for this book
is available from the British Library.

HB ISBN 978 1 444 95407 4 • PB ISBN 978 1 444 95408 1

Printed and bound in China

MIX
Paper from
responsible sources
FSC® C104740

Hodder Children's Books
An imprint of Hachette Children's Group
Part of Hodder and Stoughton
Carmelite House, 50 Victoria Embankment, London, EC4Y 0DZ

An Hachette UK Company
www.hachette.co.uk
www.hachettechildrens.co.uk

Peter Bently & Chris Jevons
Goldilocks
IN SPACE

Goldilocks was heading for space
With plenty of porridge packed up in her case.
"I'm off on a special holiday flight.
I'll find a nice planet – one that's **JUST RIGHT!**"

She hugged the Three Bears
And waved them bye-bye.
Then three, two, one – **LIFT OFF!**
She rose through the sky.

Snug in her rocket, she travelled so far,
Zooming along from star to star.
Some stars were giant . . .

and some very small.

But none of them had
any planets at all.

Goldilocks travelled from place to place . . .
And found she was totally **LOST IN SPACE!**
"I'm tired," she sighed, "and hungry too.
I'm far, far from home. Oh, what will I do?"

Then her heart gave a leap.
She saw planets ahead!
"One of them's sure to be
**JUST RIGHT!**" she said.

The first place she tried was called Planet Vlaxx . . .
But she soon found that Vlaxx was no place to relax!
She dished up some porridge, then sat on a rock . . .

And jumped up at once
with a bit of a shock!

"Ouch! My poor bottom
is burning!" she cried.
"If I stay on this planet,
I'm sure to be fried."

Then an alien said, "Is our planet
**TOO HOT?**
Try Nippity Nox.
It's a **MUCH** cooler spot!"

So Goldilocks set off for
Nippity Nox,
Where even the aliens
wore extra-thick socks.

An icicle grew on the end of her nose
As she poured out some porridge –
which instantly froze!

"This planet's **TOO COLD**!
It is not at all nice!
If I stay *here* I'll end up a
big ball of ice!"

So she climbed in her
rocket and landed at last . . .

On Planet Mahoo, which was purple and vast.
She saw some strange mountains that looked rather hairy –
That's because they were **MONSTERS**, gigantic and scary!

"Come back, tasty Earthling!" the aliens said.
Goldilocks shouted, "No way!" as she fled.
"Everything here is TOO BIG for me
And I don't want to end up an alien's tea!"

She flew to Tee-Hee
but Tee-Hee was
**TOO TINY,**

And Planet Gangoolie was
**TOO HARD** and shiny.
"It's a big ball of metal.
I can't get a grip!
This is *not* the right place
for a holiday trip!"

She tried to take off – but what rotten luck.
It was like a huge magnet. The spaceship was stuck!

She fired up the boosters
to maximum power . . .

And blasted off into an asteroid shower!

The asteroids blew her to
Hey-Diddle-Diddle.
It was nothing but gas –
she flew straight through the middle!

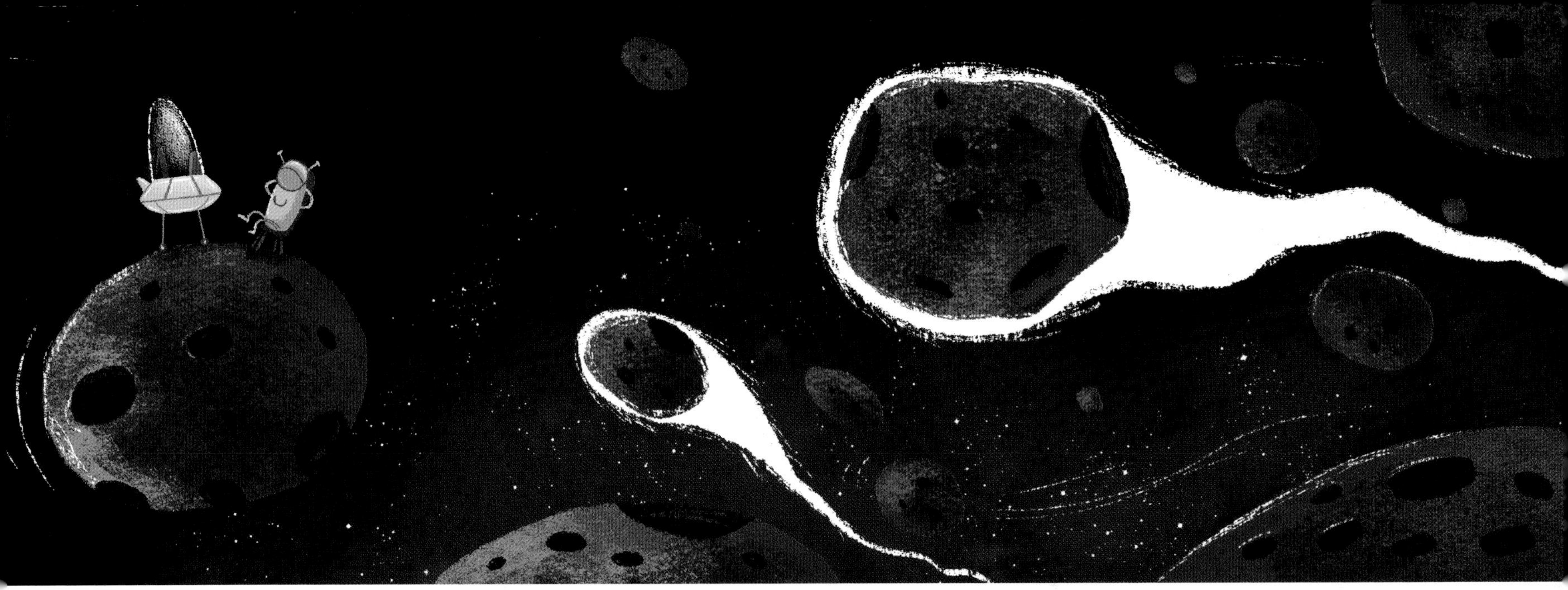

"This planet's **TOO SOFT!**
This is **NOT** the right spot!
Is there **ANY** nice planet,
not **TOO COLD** nor **TOO HOT?**

Not **TOO HARD** nor **TOO SOFT**,
not **TOO BIG** nor **TOO SMALL**,
Without any big scary monsters at all?"

"Excuse me," a voice said.
"My name is Blip,
And I know **JUST** the planet.
Follow my ship!"

Across the great cosmos the two spaceships flew
Till they came to some planets that Goldilocks knew.
As they hurtled by Mars, she said in dismay,
"I'm back where I started! We've gone the wrong way!"

"No, we haven't," said Blip,
with a chuckle of glee.
"The planet you're seeking is . . .

SLEEPING
BEAUTY
MOTEL

"… EARTH! Don't you see?"

"Not **TOO HOT**. Not **TOO COLD**. Lots of **WATER** and **AIR**.
And so many **CREATURES**! It's **AWESOME** – and **RARE**!
There are thousands of planets, but I really must say
That there's nowhere like **EARTH** in the whole Milky Way!"

"It's time for my dinner.
Bye-bye now," said Blip.
"Thank you," said Goldilocks.
"Have a good trip!
I'll finish my space journey
where I began it,
With some nice
**JUST-RIGHT** porridge . . .

"... On my own
JUST-RIGHT PLANET!"

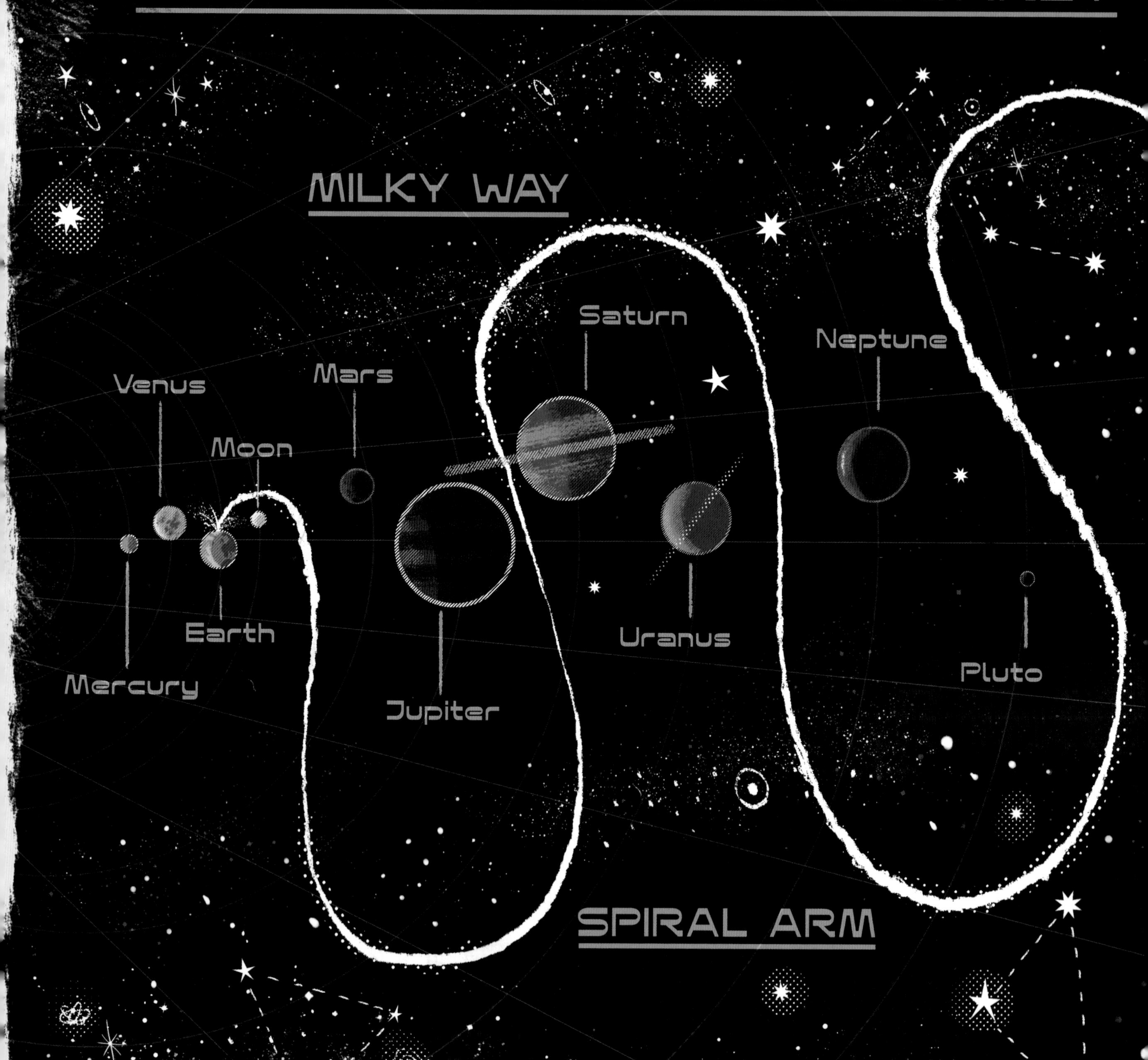
CAPTAIN GOLDILOCKS' JOURNEY
MILKY WAY
Saturn
Neptune
Venus
Mars
Moon
Earth
Uranus
Pluto
Mercury
Jupiter
SPIRAL ARM

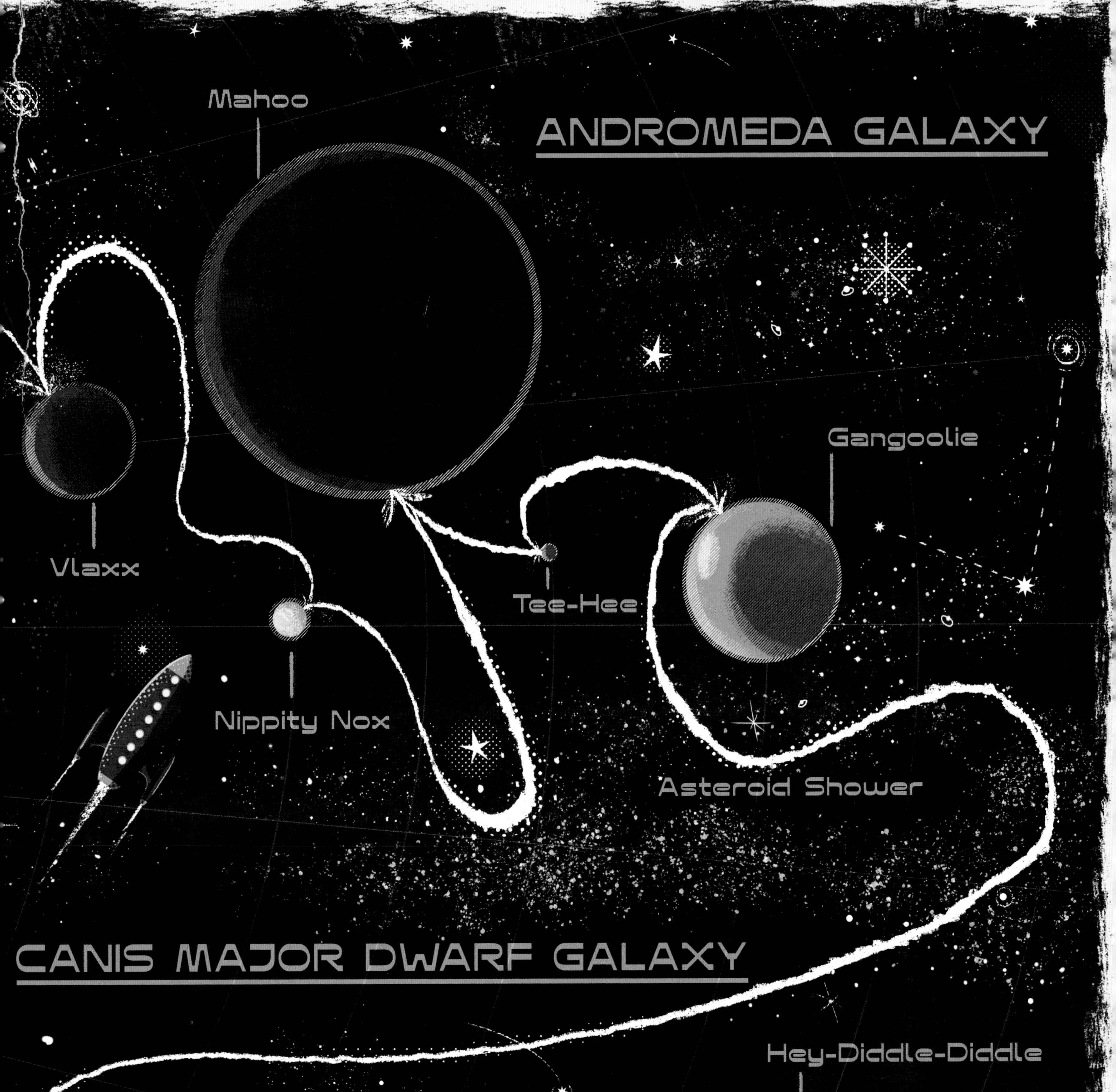
Mahoo
ANDROMEDA GALAXY
Gangoolie
Vlaxx
Tee-Hee
Nippity Nox
Asteroid Shower
CANIS MAJOR DWARF GALAXY
Hey-Diddle-Diddle

BABY BEAR
PORRIDGE